Don't Let the PEAS TOUCH!
and Other Stories

By DEBORAH BLUMENTHAL

Pictures by TIMOTHY BASIL ERING

Arthur A. Levine Books • An Imprint of Scholastic Inc.

To
Sophie and Annie
—D. B.

For Jen, my wonderful

Sophie model and critic

—T. B. E.

LIBRARY
OF CONGRESS CATALOGING-
IN-PUBLICATION DATA •
Blumenthal, Deborah. Don't let the
peas touch!/ by Deborah Blumenthal ;
illustrated by Timothy Basil Ering.   p.
cm. • Summary: In three interlinked stories,
sisters Annie and Sophie argue over such issues
as foods touching on a plate, quiet time, and pet
ownership. ISBN 0-439-29732-X   • [1.
Sisters—Fiction.] I. Title: Don't let the peas
touch!. II. Ering, Timothy B., ill. III. Title. •
PZ7.B6267Do   2004   [E]—dc22
2003021269   1 3 5 7 9 10 8
6   4   2   04 05 06
07 08

Printed
in Singapore   46
First edition, October 2004
The type was set in 16-point
Hadriano Light, 21-point Coop
Flaired and 25-point Melanie. The art
for this book was created using
graphite pencil, grease pencil, ink
pen, and acrylic paint on paper.
Book design by Kristina
Albertson

Text
copyright © 2004 by
Deborah   Blumenthal   •
Illustrations copyright © 2004 by Timothy
Basil Ering • All rights reserved. Published
by Arthur A. Levine Books, an imprint of
Scholastic Inc., Publishers since 1920. SCHOLASTIC
and the LANTERN LOGO are trademarks and/or
registered trademarks of Scholastic Inc. • No part of
this publication may be reproduced, or stored in a
retrieval system, or transmitted in any form or by any
means, electronic, mechanical, photocopying,
recording, or otherwise, without written permission of the publisher. For information regard-
ing permission, write to Scholastic Inc.,
Attention: Permissions Department,
557 Broadway, New York,
NY 10012.

Don't Let the
PEAS TOUCH!

Sophie's big sister Annie was taking a cooking class.
And this weekend, she was supposed to help make all
the family's meals.

But every time Sophie sat down to eat, something was wrong on her plate. At breakfast, milk was in her cereal when she didn't want it there. So she held her nose with one hand while she drained off the milk with the other. Then she sifted through the cereal to screen out a raisin.

"Do you like the pit part?" Sophie asked her father.

He rolled his eyes. "A raisin doesn't have a pit. Just eat the whole thing."

"Never mind, the raisins are a nice touch, Annie," said their mother.

She glared at Sophie, but Sophie was too busy doing raisin surgery to notice.

At lunch, Annie made everyone roast beef sandwiches.

Sophie opened hers and held up squares of meat in front of the window.

"What are you doing now?" her mother asked.

"Looking for fat," Sophie said.

"There's no fat," her mother said. "Annie cut off all the fat."

"Not this," Sophie said, shaking a zigzag of gristle. She balled up the meat and hid it under her plate.

"You're **SSOO GROSS**," Annie yelled at Sophie.

"Am **NOT!**" Sophie yelled back.

"ARE TOO!" Annie screamed.

"Stop!" their mother said. "Both of you!"

For dinner, Annie said she was going to make something that **everyone** would love. She waved her arms around and said, "Tonight I will prepare a special recipe from a French cookbook!"

Everyone waited and waited until Annie finally came out of the kitchen. She was wearing the tallest hat that Sophie had ever seen. In her hand was a big pan.

Annie lifted the lid high up into the air, then bowed
and said, "Ze best blue cheese omelet!"

"Ooh la la," their mother said. She took a forkful.
"Just delicious," she said in a television voice, blowing
Annie a kiss.

With his mouth full, their father saluted Annie.
"Magnifique!"

But Sophie just waved Annie away. "Eeeewwww, don't give me any of **THAT**," she said, draping a napkin over her head. "It's *sssoooo* stinky."

Annie pushed her face next to Sophie's. "There's no cheese in your omelet. None **what-so-ever**."

Annie put the plain omelet in front of Sophie with a flourish.

For a moment, everything was calm. Then Annie served the side dish.

"Oh **NO!**" Sophie yelled. "The peas are **TOUCHING**
the eggs! Don't let them touch!"

"So what if they touch?" Annie yelled, breathing
on Sophie. **"THEY MIX IN YOUR STOMACH ANYWAY!"**

She shoved the peas away, but they rolled back.

Annie grabbed French bread, wedging it between the eggs and the peas. "I **HATE** that bread . . . all the crust!" Sophie yelled, bumping her glass and sending a wave of water over the table.

"Eeeeeewww," Sophie said, as a pea-juice puddle drowned the bread, turning it green and soggy, floating all the food together.

Her father shook his head. "Just terrible," he muttered.

No one spoke for a long time. Then suddenly, Annie pounded the table with her fist.

"**AHA!**" she shouted.

She ran to the kitchen and climbed a ladder, coming down
with a box. Inside it was a strange dish. It was a big dish that
held little dishes. Ten of them. And each one had walls! Best
of all, it turned like a wheel.

Annie held it out to Sophie like a present. "Some call it a lazy Susan. We'll call it — a *separator*."

So for the rest of the weekend, Annie helped Sophie separate frozen strawberries from strawberry ice cream, white icing from brown sandwich cookies, even peanut butter from jelly.

And everything tasted a little better that way.

Sssssssssssssshhhhhhhhh!
IT'S QUIET TIME!

The next weekend, Sophie and Annie went to the zoo. They laughed and laughed watching the monkeys doing circus tricks in their cages.

But when they got home, Annie told Sophie that they were going to have quiet time.

"What's that?" Sophie asked.

"Quiet time is when you have fun playing quietly, all by yourself," Annie said.

Then she sat on the couch with her recipe book.

Sophie stood in the middle of the room, unsure of what to do.

Then she took a book out too and sat down next to Annie.

She flipped one page and tried to make out the words.

But she needed a little help getting started.

"What does this say?" she asked softly.

Annie glanced at the book. "The giraffe says, 'I have to stop talking, I have a sore throat.'"

Sophie nodded and flipped the page. She stared and stared, trying to figure out what that giraffe was going to do next.

But she couldn't.

"Annie!" Sophie said. "I don't know what this says either!"

Annie drew a hard finger up to her lips. "We'll read later, just look at the pictures."

"Okay," Sophie mouthed. "Okay."

Sophie tiptoed out of the room. Reading was too noisy for quiet time, but she knew that Annie would like it if she got herself a snack.

She crept over to the kitchen and carefully plucked a green apple from a bowl on the table. She pulled the chair out. **SKKKKQUEAK!** Then she pulled herself up to the table. **SCCCCRRRRAAAPE!** Finally she took a big bite.

CRUNCH. CRUNCH CRUNCH. "Mmmmmm."

CRUNCH, CRUNCH, CRUNCH. "MmmmMMMMM!"

"**SOPHIE!**" Annie snapped. "I'm trying to study."

"Sorry!" Sophie whispered.
"I'll go play a quiet game. You
won't even know I'm here."

Sophie went into her room and came back dragging a carton of blocks.

"I'm making a circus," Sophie said.

"By yourself," Annie said, picking up her book again. "**QUI-ET-LY.**"

First Sophie made a long line of blocks, laying them down carefully, one by one. Then she covered it with animals. "And now, ladies and gentlemen," Sophie announced in a breathy whisper, "dogs, cats, birds, and wild creatures from all over the world will march in!" Sophie took the creatures two by two and paraded them in to a quiet little song.

"La dee do dah, la dee dum, DUM de Dum de DUM DUM."

Then she made the audience give them a quiet cheer.

"Wooooooooooooohooooooooo Yaaaaaaaaaaayyyyy!"

"**SSSSSSSSSSHHHHHHHHHHHHH!**" Annie hissed.

Sophie held two animals up mid-march. "Okay, I know.

I'll build a quiet place where all my tired animals can sleep."

"Perfect," Annie said, snuggling up to her book.

So Sophie started to build a very quiet, very tall sleeping house. After she had the first floor built, she lowered the animals down onto beds one by one. Then she built the walls up high, high, high so that no sound could come in to disturb them. Finally, she grabbed some pillows from the couch to lay over the blocks for a roof. All she needed was one last heavy one to keep out every possible sound, but . . .

Annie jumped up.
"I CAN'T TAKE IT!"
she yelled.

"**SSSHHH!**" Sophie said, wagging her finger. "You'll wake up the animals. It's QUIET time."

The SURPRISE Pet

Sophie wanted a pet. A special pet all her own that she could love and take care of. But whenever she asked her parents for a pet, they always said no.

"We have Bluebell," her mother said. "One pet is enough."

But Bluebell was Annie's pet.

"Share Bluebell," their mother tried.

"How can you share a pet?" Sophie said. "You can't cut it in half like a pickle."

Annie smiled. "You **should** get Sophie a pet," she said.

"See?" Sophie said.

Their mother raised her eyebrows.

"Yes," Annie said, "but not just any pet. **A BIG, FAT PIG** that would eat everything that she left over."

Annie laughed and laughed.

"Be quiet, Annie," Sophie said.

Annie kept on laughing, slapping her knee.

Sophie bolted from her chair. She raced up the stairs to her room. The door slammed. **BOOM!**

Their mother and father looked at Annie, shaking their
heads. "I didn't mean it," Annie said softly, looking down.
Annie climbed the stairs to Sophie's room.
Outside the door, Annie said it again. "I didn't mean it."
"Okay," said a whispery voice.

Annie went in and sat on the bed.

"I'm sorry," Annie said, "so I'm going to get you a real pet."

"What kind?" Sophie said.

"It's a *surprise*," Annie said. "For us to share."

The next day, Sophie waited and waited for Annie to come home from school.

"What's in the bag?" Sophie said. "Is it my pet?"

"Maybe," Annie said, smiling. She opened the bag.

She took out a plastic cup. Sophie didn't see anything in it.

"Where is it?" she said, squinting. "I don't see a pet."

"It's there," Annie said. "It's a seed."

"A seed?" Sophie said. "It's so tiny. We're going to *share* it?"

"I'll show you how," Annie said.

"We can both sing quietly to it and carry it around."

"Me first," said Sophie.

Annie rolled her eyes.

"But we have to treat it carefully," Annie said. "It's a living thing."

"I'll be careful," Sophie said, grabbing the cup. "Here, seed. Here, Tiny."

When their mother saw Tiny, she smiled.

"What a cute little pet," she said, "so well behaved."

Sophie showed Tiny
her room, her toys,
her favorite bear.

The whole house.

She showed him Annie's room too,
but faster.

When Sophie's friend Rachel came over, Sophie showed her Tiny. Rachel looked and looked into the cup.

"There's no pet in there," Rachel said. "Is dirt a pet?"

"Tiny's there," Sophie said. "Only special people like me and my big sister know that."

"Oh," said Rachel, "I think I see him now. Yes, I can see him."

But sometimes when Sophie was alone, she began to
think that maybe Rachel was right. Tiny didn't bark.
He didn't meow. He didn't chirp. He didn't nip her fingers.
He didn't eat. Maybe he wasn't even alive. She began to cry.

"Why are you crying, Sophie?" Annie asked.

"Because we don't **really** have a pet," Sophie said.
"We can't even see him."

"That doesn't mean he's not real," Annie said. "He still
needs our love and strong thoughts. Can you give him that?"

"Yes," Sophie said. "I can."

"Good," Annie said. "So can I."

At bedtime, Sophie put Tiny on her night table. In the moonlight, she watched him and watched him. Nothing happened. She closed her eyes and thought hard about Tiny changing and growing, and becoming more and more of what he could be.

In the morning, the sun was shining. Sophie looked into Tiny's cup. Her eyes opened wide.

"Annie! Annie!" she shouted. "**COME LOOK!**"

Annie ran in and looked into the cup. A small green leaf sprouted from the tiny seed. Tiny wasn't just a seed anymore. "Tiny turned into a little plant!" Sophie said.

"Yes," Annie said, planting a tiny kiss on Sophie's head.
"That's life."